These are the adventures of a lively leprechaun,

He's from the west of Ireland, his name is Shamrock Sean.

He has a little bushy beard, his hair is thick and grey.

He's older than the Blarney Stone if he's a single day.

He loves to eat potatoes – boiled or mashed or roast,

But cabbage mixed with bacon is what he loves the most.

He lives inside a toadstool, beneath a tree of oak,

And if you wander Knock-Na-Shee you might

see his chimney smoke.

Shamrock Sean went fishing

Down by the river's edge.

His rod was just a little stick

He'd found beside the hedge.

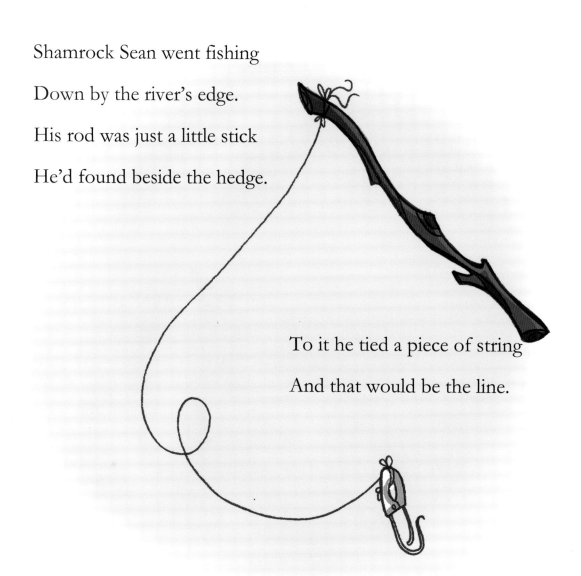

To it he tied a piece of string

And that would be the line.

His hook was just a safety pin,

But it would do just fine.

Shamrock Sean
Goes Fishing

Brian Gogarty

Illustrated by Roxanne Burchartz
of The Cartoon Saloon

THE O'BRIEN PRESS
DUBLIN

For my wife, Eileen, and children Christine,
Nuala and Ryan, because they believe ...

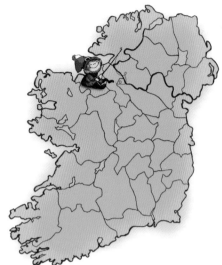

First published 2007 by The O'Brien Press Ltd.
12 Terenure Road East, Rathgar, Dublin 6, Ireland.
Tel: +353 1 4923333; Fax: +353 1 4922777
E-mail: books@obrien.ie
Website: www.obrien.ie

ISBN: 978-0-86278-968-8

British Library Cataloguing-in-Publication Data
Gogarty, Brian
Shamrock Sean goes fishing
1. Shamrock Sean (Fictitious character) - Pictorial works -Juvenile fiction
2. Fishing - Pictorial works - Juvenile fiction 3. Children's stories - Pictorial works
I. Title
823.9'2[J]

1 2 3 4 5 6
07 08 09 10

The O'Brien Press receives assistance from

Editing, typesetting and design: The O'Brien Press Ltd
Printing: Leo Paper Products Ltd

He put the stick between two stones,

He fixed it firm and tight.

Then lay down in the summer sun

And waited for a bite.

After many hours of waiting

The rod began to twitch.

Shamrock Sean said to himself –

This must be one big fish!

Or could it be a heavy boot?

Or might it be a rag?

But then he saw the safety pin

Had hooked a leather bag.

He opened up the bag

And could not believe his eyes.

For it was full of precious gems,

What a great surprise!

He put his hand into the bag

And moved it all about.

He found a note and trembled

As he read the message out:

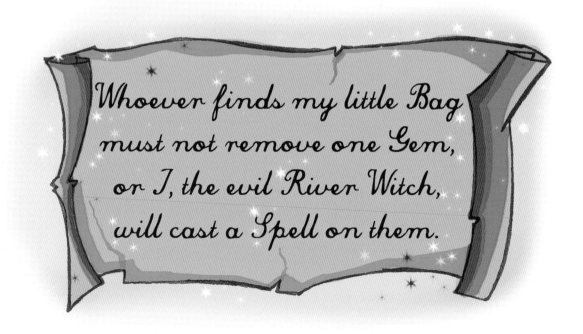

Whoever finds my little Bag
must not remove one Gem,
or I, the evil River Witch,
will cast a Spell on them.

Shamrock Sean is honest,

So he closed the bag up tight

And threw it back into the stream

With all his strength and might.

It hit the water with a splash

As he fell upon the ground.

Then a big fish grabbed his foot

And dragged him river-bound.

'Let me go,' cried Shamrock Sean.

He flapped his arms and screamed.

Then suddenly he woke up –

It had all been just a dream.

On the soft grass, in the sun,

Upon the bank so steep,

He'd rolled into the water

When he'd fallen fast asleep.

He crawled out of the water

And the rod began to twitch.

'Oh no!' he cried as he ran home.

'Here comes the River Witch!'